The Common Cold

By Sally Cowan

Contents

Why We Catch a Cold

The common cold is caused by a tiny virus. The virus lives inside the human body, in the nose and throat. But it can also survive for a short time outside the body.

the cold virus, seen with a microscope

A cold makes fluid drip from the nose. The fluid is full of the virus. People catch colds when the virus spreads from one person to another.

People with colds get the virus on their hands when blowing or wiping their nose, or covering their sneezes. The virus can then be passed on to others by touch; for example, by holding or shaking hands.

Key

virus

The virus can also be left on things such as phones, money or even door handles. When other people touch these things, they get the virus on their hands.

When someone with a cold coughs or sneezes, droplets of the virus can spread into the air. Anyone who comes into contact with those droplets may catch a cold.

Once people have the virus on their hands, they might touch their face. The virus can enter the body through the nose, mouth or eyes.

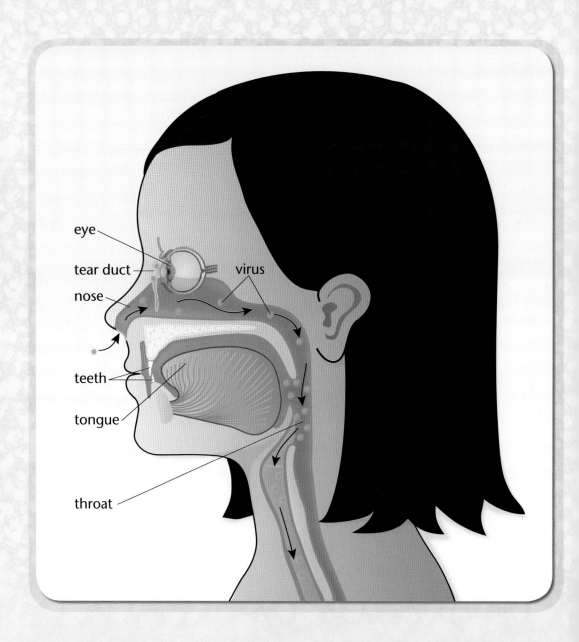

eye

tear duct

nose

virus

teeth

tongue

throat

After entering the body, the virus travels quickly to the back of the throat, where it starts to multiply.

About a day after the virus enters someone's body, that person begins to feel unwell. The cold often starts with a sore throat, followed by sneezing and fluid dripping from the nose.

Green Valley School Newsletter

No Colds for Our School!

By Kyle Jarvis, Year 5

Every winter, many students at our school get sick with colds. The cold virus spreads quickly and easily from person to person.

I believe our school can be a much healthier place this winter. Everyone needs to take more responsibility for their own health and think about keeping other students healthy, too.

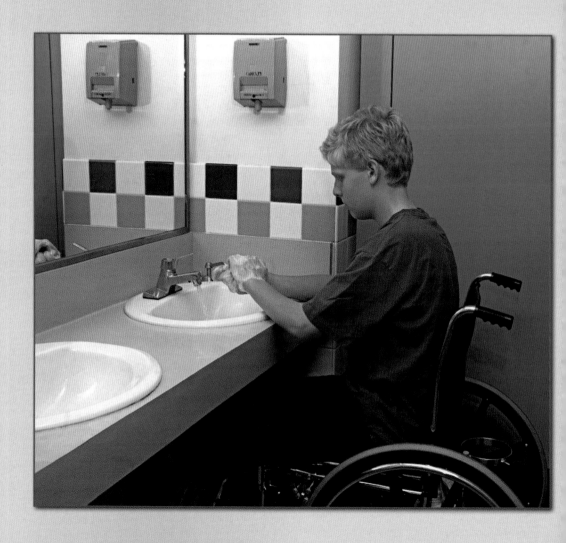

First, students could easily stop the cold virus from spreading if they wash and dry their hands often and thoroughly. They should also try not to touch their eyes, nose or mouth. Then they can avoid infecting themselves with any virus that they may have come into contact with.

Second, it is very important to eat fresh, healthy foods. But students should not share food with each other, especially if they have a cold.

Third, students should exercise every day. The health nurse explained to everyone at assembly that people who exercise get fewer colds.

Finally, all students should get plenty of sleep every night. Tired people are more likely to catch a cold.

If students do catch a cold, they must be sure to stay at home until they are well again. Then they won't spread the virus.

Everyone should carry tissues, which should be put in a bin after use. Or if students have to sneeze suddenly, they should sneeze into their arm to stop the virus from spreading into the air.

If students all make these simple changes, our school will be a much healthier place this winter.

No Colds for Our School!

Wash and dry your hands thoroughly.

Eat healthy foods and don't share food.

Exercise every day.

Get plenty of sleep.

Stay home if you are sick.

Use tissues or your arm to catch sneezes.